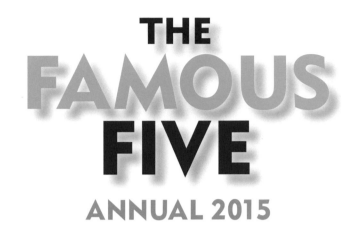

THE FAMOUS FIVE

ANNUAL 2015

BOOKS IN THE FAMOUS FIVE SERIES

All available from Hodder Children's Books

Enid Blyton

THE
FAMOUS
FIVE
ANNUAL 2015

Hodder Children's Books

A division of Hachette Children's Books

With special thanks, once again, to Tony Summerfield of the
Enid Blyton Society for advice and contributions to this book.
For more information about the Famous Five, Enid Blyton
and her books, visit the website of the Enid Blyton Society at
www.enidblytonsociety.co.uk.

The acknowledgements on p. 64 constitute an extension of
this copyright notice
Enid Blyton's signature is a Registered Trade Mark of
Hodder & Stoughton Ltd.

First published in Great Britain in 2014 by
Hodder Children's Books

A Catalogue record for this book is available from the
British Library

ISBN 978 1 444 918816

Book design by Janette Revill
Printed and bound in China by WKT

The paper and board used in this hardback by Hodder Children's
Books are natural recyclable products made from wood grown in
sustainable forests. The manufacturing processes conform to the
environmental regulations of the country of origin.

Hodder Children's Books
a division of Hachette Children's Books
338 Euston Road, London NW1 3BH
An Hachette UK company

www.hachette.co.uk

CONTENTS

WHO ARE THE FAMOUS FIVE?

ANNE

The youngest of the Five. She's a small, pretty girl. Despite the fact that she sometimes finds adventures just a bit too thrilling, you try stopping her going along! Anne is tidy and organised: there's nothing she likes better than setting up a neat camp. Without her, the Five would probably never bother to eat properly...

DICK

Julian's younger brother. He's not as wise as Julian and is inclined to fall headlong into danger. He's a little zany and full of fun; but bright, enthusiastic and always ready to help. Certainly very good company for anyone who loves adventure!

JULIAN

The eldest of the Five and the brother of Anne and Dick. Julian may not be a grown-up, but he often appears that way to the others. Although he loves the excitement of their many adventures, he always behaves responsibly and looks after the group. Most importantly, he always knows when a mystery is getting too hot to handle and it's time to call in the police!

GEORGE

The girl with her very own island —Kirrin Island, where the Five spend a good deal of their holidays. George is the cousin of Julian, Dick and Anne. With her mop of curly hair and dislike of dresses, she's usually mistaken for a boy; and if you want to see one of her famous scowls, just call her by her real name—Georgina!

TIMMY George's loveable mongrel dog, who goes everywhere with her—even to school! Very intelligent, he has a tail-wagging welcome for people he likes, but he can snap and snarl like a guard-dog when the Five are in danger.

MEET THE BADDIES

In last year's Annual we met the Five's friends. But these wouldn't be true adventures without the baddies to stand in the Five's way. Here's an introduction to some of them …

Lewis Allburg (*Five Go Off in a Caravan*): Known to his friends as Lou, Lewis Allburg works in Mr Gorgio's circus. He is a fine acrobat who can 'climb anything anywhere'. Like so many of the villains encountered by the Five, Lou has a revolver with which he threatens to kill Timmy. Lou and his partner, **Tiger Dan**, rob rich houses and hide their loot in the **Merran Hills**.

Mr Barling (*Five Go to Smuggler's Top*): A smuggler who lives on **Castaway Hill** and is determined that the marshes will not be drained. He kidnaps Quentin Kirrin and Pierre Lenoir. He knows the hidden paths across the marshes around Castaway Hill and uses them to bring smuggled goods into the country from small ships anchored out at sea. The local police believe that he is involved in smuggling but he is a clever man and manages to escape detection. After his encounter with the Five he becomes lost in the honeycomb of passages that run through Castaway Hill and Timmy has to help the police rescue him and some of his men. Like so many of the other villains encountered by the Five, he carries a gun.

Block (*Five Go to Smuggler's Top*): We never learn what Block's first name is but we do know that he is a sly, unpleasant character. He works as a servant for **Mr Lenoir** at **Smuggler's Top** but is actually there as a spy for **Mr Barling**, the smuggler. Block pretends to be deaf and in this way overhears all sorts of private information which he reports back to his boss. He always wears the same white linen coat and black trousers. He is as strong as a horse and once he realises that the children suspect him of villainy he takes every opportunity he can to be unpleasant to them.

'Tiger' Dan (*Five Go Off in a Caravan*): Dan is the chief clown at Mr Gorgio's circus but the Five have never met anyone less like a clown than the bad-tempered, bullying Dan. When they first meet him he is dirty, shabbily dressed and chewing on an old pipe. He angrily orders them to move their caravans away from the circus camp but is even more furious later when he discovers the Five are camping in the hills above Lake Merran. Dan is a brutal man who cruelly treats any animals or circus folk who get in his way. He knocks out **Pongo**, the circus chimpanzee, with a stone, and threatens to poison Timmy. He makes out that he is **Nobby**'s uncle but in fact he is not related to the boy. Tiger Dan and his friend **Lou** use their circus work as a cover for stealing priceless valuables. Their plan is to eventually take their plunder to Holland, where Dan once worked, and sell it.

Block

Tiger Dan

Gringo *(Five Have Plenty of Fun)*: Owner of 'Gringo's Great Fair' and prepared to do anything if a wad of money is offered to him. According to **Spiky**, the roundabout boy, Gringo pays his workers well but drives them like slaves. He is fond of his own comforts and has a double caravan where he lives with his old mother. He also owns a large silver-grey and blue American car. Gringo is responsible for kidnapping George (thinking she is **Berta Wright**) and keeping her in a cistern room in a house in the village of Twining.

The Guv'nor *(Five Go Down to the Sea)*: Leader of the **Barnies**. The Guv'nor is a small man who rarely smiles and is obsessed with looking after the head of **Clopper**, the pantomime horse. He uses the contacts he makes while travelling around Cornwall to organise drug smuggling.

Junior Henning *(Five On Finniston Farm)*: The spoilt and selfish American boy staying with his father at **Finniston Farm**. Junior is about eleven years old, never lifts a finger to help if he can avoid it and never bothers to say 'please' or 'thank you'. He leaves his room in a mess and expects breakfast in bed. He finds out the Five's plans by eavesdropping.

Mr Henning *(Five On Finniston Farm)*: A man intent on buying up every antique he can find at knock-down prices. He contemplates making an offer for the chapel at Finniston Farm and taking it back to the USA! Like his son, Junior, Mr Henning has a cunning streak and when he learns that treasures are possibly buried under Finniston Farm he tries to get the owner of the farm to sign a contract that will result in the American getting any finds at a bargain price.

Will Janes *(Five Go to Billycock Hill)*: A burly man with a thick neck who once worked on Billycock Farm before going to live with his old mother on the Butterfly Farm where she is housekeeper to Mr Gringle and Mr Brent. Will has fallen in with bad company and gives shelter to a group of men who plan to steal two top-secret fighter planes from the Air Force base close to **Billycock Hill**. He has a violent and dangerous temper and is very much a bully.

Johnson *(Five On Kirrin Island Again)*: Johnson, a former colleague of Quentin Kirrin, is one of three villains who try to steal Quentin Kirrin's secret new fuel. Johnson and his partner, Peters, parachute down onto Kirrin Island, take Quentin prisoner and shut Timmy into a small underground cave. They not only try to steal the formula but also threaten to blow up the entire island!

Ebenezer and Jacob Loomer *(Five Go to Demon's Rocks)*: Descended from 'Wreckers' who used to lure ships onto Demon's Rocks so that they could steal their valuable cargoes, Ebenezer and Jacob now try to earn their living showing visitors around the Wreckers Cave. For years they have searched unsuccessfully for the treasure of gold, silver and pearls believed to have been hidden in the cave by their ancestor, One-Ear Bill. When the Five and **Tinker** leave the key in the lock of **Demon's Rocks Lighthouse** Jacob not only goes in and steals valuables but also removes the key and later uses it to trap the children in the lighthouse.

Ebeneezer and Jacob

Maggie Martin (*Five On a Hike Together*):
A tall woman with a sharp and determined voice whom the children thought looked as hard as nails when they encountered her and **Dirty Dick** at **Two Trees** while on the trail of stolen jewels. The pair were no match for the Five when it came to working out the location of the stolen jewels.

Mr Perton and gang (*Five Get Into Trouble*):
Owner of Owl's Dene and leader of a desperate group of villains who, amongst other things, hide escaped convicts from the police. His gang includes Hunchy, Ben and Fred. No guns are actually displayed but Mr Perton does threaten to shoot Timmy.

Jeffrey Pottersham (*Five Have a Wonderful Time*):
A scientist who not only wants to sell his secrets to a foreign power but also kidnaps Derek Terry-Kane with the intention of making him divulge his secrets. Pottersham is fascinated by old ruins (he has written a book on the subject) and his knowledge of the secret passages hidden inside the walls of Faynights Castle allows him to find the perfect hiding place for his victim while he waits to take him across the Channel to Europe. Like so many of the villains encountered by the Five, Pottersham threatens Timmy with a gun.

Rooky (*Five Get Into Trouble*):
Ex-bodyguard to Thurlow Kent and a bad tempered bully. Rooky has a violent temper and scares everyone at Owl's Dene where he is involved in a number of illegal plots. He threatens the Five when they arrive at Owl's Dene looking for Richard Kent, and tries to have Timmy poisoned after the dog bites him.

Mr Roland and friends (*Five Go Adventuring Again*):
A clever villain is a dangerous villain, and Mr Roland, who comes to Kirrin Cottage as a tutor for Julian, Dick and George, is a very clever man. Not only does he have an excellent knowledge of all the subjects on the children's school curriculum, he also has a good understanding of Quentin Kirrin's secret work. He has a dry manner of speaking and while he pretends to be very friendly towards Julian, Dick and Anne he goes out of his way to upset George. However, this is just a clever way of getting George into trouble and Timothy out of the house. Mr Roland claims that since being bitten by a dog as a boy he dislikes them, but his real fear is that Timothy, whose ears are even sharper than Mr Roland's eyes, will hear him searching Quentin's laboratory for the secret formula he intends to steal and warn the household.

Sniffer's father (*Five Go to Mystery Moor*):
We never learn the name of Sniffer's father but we do know that he is not a pleasant man. He treats **Sniffer** badly and ill-treats his horse, **Clip**. He appears to be the leader of a gang receiving forged hundred-dollar notes, flown over from France and dropped by plane onto a lonely stretch of **Mystery Moor**. He, or one of his gang, knock out Timmy, capture Anne and George and tie them up in a cave in the centre of a hill.

Mr Roland

The Stick Family (*Five Run Away Together*): About the only good things that can be said about Clara Stick is that she is fond of her dog, **Tinker**, and is a very good cook. She comes to Kirrin Cottage to take the place of **Joanna** who has to leave in a hurry to look after her sick mother. Mrs Stick is a sour-faced woman who is quick to grumble and easily upset. When made angry by the Five she refuses to make cakes for tea, and when Uncle Quentin leaves to take Aunt Fanny to hospital Mrs Stick tries to keep the children very short of food. She is afraid of Timmy and attempts to poison his food. When she and her husband kidnap **Jennifer Armstrong** she shows no remorse that they have shut the small, frightened girl up in a dark and terrifying place. Mrs Stick is a very unpleasant woman.

Her son, Edgar, is a youth of thirteen or fourteen. He is an unpleasant tell-tale, always on the lookout to play sly tricks on the Five but quick to tell his mother if they try to retaliate. He annoys George by singing silly songs about her but runs away when Julian makes a step

towards him. Edgar has a wide, red, pimply face with screwed up eyes and a long nose. Julian and the others call him Spotty Face. He gets little attention from his parents and is probably an unhappy child.

Mr Stick is a seaman on leave from his ship. He is dirty and unkempt but displays good skills of seamanship as he manoeuvres a boat through the dangerous rocks that surround Kirrin Island. He has come to Kirrin to take part in a kidnap plot for which he is to be well paid. He carries a gun and seems quite prepared to use it.

The fourth member of the Stick family is Sarah, a maid working at the Armstrong house who helps to arrange for Jenny Armstrong to be kidnapped.

Llewellyn Thomas (*Five Get Into a Fix*): The wayward son of Bronwen Thomas who has faked his own murder and imprisoned his mother in the tower room of **Old Towers** so that he can mine and sell the valuable metal that is buried under Old Towers Hill.

Red Tower and his gang (*Five Fall Into Adventure*): Red Tower lives in a castle-like building at **Port Limmersley** and is responsible for organising the kidnapping of George and Timmy. He hopes to exchange George for the notebooks containing Quentin Kirrin's latest research work. To look at he is a giant of a man with flaming red hair, eyebrows and beard. Red has mad tempers and takes cruel revenge on anyone who crosses him. He threatens his own men with a gun and tells them: 'my orders are always obeyed!' His chief henchman is Markhoff, a short and burly fellow who carries a gun and is only just prevented from shooting Timmy. Other men working for Red are Simmy (the father of **Jo**), Jake, Carl and Tom.

Dirty Dick (Taggart) (*Five On a Hike Together*): An unpleasant character who lives with his mother in a tumbledown cottage on the moors. He has broad shoulders, a shock of untidy hair and a dreadful temper. With the aid of **Maggie Martin** he hopes to find the jewels stolen from the Queen of Fallonia and hidden near **Two Trees**. However, he is beaten to this prize by the Five, who see that the jewels are taken to the police for safe return to their owner. Dirty Dick comes to a really sticky end when he is stuck in a marsh with a broken ankle.

FIVE GO TO BILLYCOCK HILL

You'll need to look at the list of chapters in the sixteenth adventure to find the words that fit into this grid. We've put the numbers below as a list of clues – and have started you off with five famous letters!

ACROSS
1. See chapter 2
6. See chapter 15
7. See chapter 18
9. See chapter 20
12. See chapter 12
13. See chapter 4
14. See chapter 11
17. See chapter 5
19. See chapter 7
20. See chapter 5
21. See chapter 6

DOWN
2. See chapter 18
3. See chapter 7
4. See chapter 12
5. See chapter 8
8. See chapter 7
10. See chapter 15
11. See chapter18
12. See chapter 4
15. See chapter 14
16. See chapter 9
18. See chapter 16

THE FAMOUS FIVE ON TV

There has been a Famous Five play, a musical and also two film serials, but perhaps the best-known adaptations are the TV series.

In 1978, *The Famous Five*, made by Southern Television, was screened by ITV. There were two seasons, containing a total of twenty-six episodes, each of thirty minutes. Eighteen of the books were adapted – the rights for *Five On a Treasure Island* and *Five Have a Mystery to Solve* belonged elsewhere, and *Five Have Plenty of Fun* couldn't be included in the production schedule.

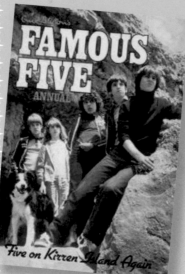

The actors who played the Five wore contemporary clothes so it was cast as a modern-day adventure series.

In 1979, Hodder & Stoughton reissued the first six Famous Five books in large format hardback editions liberally illustrated with stills from the TV series. Before and after the TV series was shown, Purnell published annuals, inspired by the programme (but they also contained new line drawings and other activities).

The first TV series was so successful that it is rumoured that the producers wanted to generate new storylines for another, but this was opposed by Darrell Waters Limited (the Estate of Enid Blyton). The series has been screened many times on TV and was packaged as videos and DVDs.

In 1995, the series was remade by Zenith North, with the actors wearing clothes of the 1940s and 1950s. This time, all the books were dramatized.

There was an annual for the 1990s series, but the only DVD issued in the UK was *Five On a Treasure Island*. Boxed sets were released in several European countries, but the Dutch edition (which most people buy) is missing *Five Go to Smuggler's Top*. Boxed sets of the 1970s series are also available.

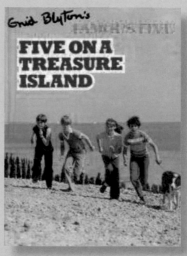

1990s

1970s

14

15

19

MEET EILEEN SOPER

As the original illustrator of the Famous Five, for many people Eileen Soper's name will always be associated with that of Enid Blyton. What is perhaps not so widely known is that over a twenty-one year period she illustrated well over a hundred books for Blyton and this included over sixty instantly recognisable dust jackets. When she started illustrating children's books in the early 1940s, however, she was already recognised as a gifted artist on both sides of the Atlantic.

Eileen Alice Soper was born in Enfield, North London on 26 March 1905, the second daughter of George and Ada Soper. Her elder sister, Eva, was born in March 1901. George Soper was an artist best known for his etchings and watercolours of horses. When Eileen was three, the family moved to a new house at Harmer Green in what was then rural Hertfordshire, a house that Eileen and Eva were to live in for the rest of their lives as neither of them ever married. George had bought a large plot of land and helped to design the house which included a large studio. Eileen and Eva went to a small private school in Knebworth run by Olive Downing and later to Hitchin Girls School.

Eileen did not enjoy school and it was at home that her artistic talents started to flourish under the strong guidance of her father. She longed to follow in her father's footsteps and from an early age she often had a pencil in her hand. She made her first etching when she was thirteen and a year later her father sent four of her prints to an exhibition in Los Angeles where they were much admired. In the spring of 1921, two of these, 'The Broken Gate' and 'The Swing' were exhibited at the Royal Academy in London and at the age of fifteen Eileen became the Academy's youngest ever exhibitor. Suddenly Eileen was famous and her prints were exhibited on both sides of the Atlantic over the next few years. Her favourite subject was children at play and one of her prints was bought by Queen Mary in 1924 which further enhanced her reputation.

During the 1930s the popularity of etchings waned, so when Eileen was approached by Macmillan in 1941 and asked if she would illustrate three readers for Enid Blyton she readily accepted, and a new door opened for her. Eileen had always enjoyed writing herself and after three years of illustrating books for Enid

Blyton, including a series of picture books for Brockhampton Press, she thought it would be nice if she could illustrate her own books for children. Her first book, *Happy Rabbit*, was accepted by Macmillan as were two further books in the same series, but sales dropped on the third book and Macmillan rejected her fourth book. She tried a number of other publishers and wrote and illustrated a further four books in the series, but failed to find a publisher. She then decided to turn her attention to poetry and after several rejections she did eventually get *Songs of the Wind* published by the Museum Press, but it didn't sell well and she had developed a reputation as a difficult author to work with, so this marked the end of her writing for children.

now an invalid. Eva went into a nursing home and a while later with her health starting to fail, Eileen joined her. She died on 18 March 1990, a few days before her eighty-fifth birthday and Eva also died a few months later in the same year.

She heaved a sigh of relief, and began to row strongly away from the shore (see page 131)

Despite her writing difficulties her illustrating had gone from strength to strength, and as well as Blyton she worked on books by several other authors including a series of farm and countryside books for Elizabeth Gould, all of which contained some magnificent colour plates. She was also illustrating all the merchandise for the Famous Five and this included twenty jigsaws for BesTime. To go with a series of thirty nature readers, she also produced sixty colour posters which were delightfully illustrated and are still sought after today.

After her final book for Blyton in 1963, Eileen turned her attention to her love of wildlife and wrote and illustrated several books about the animals in what was now a virtually wild garden. At the same time she was looking after her sister who was

FOOD IN THE FAMOUS FIVE

From their first appearance in print, the Famous Five put away their fair share of villains and ne'er-do-wells, as well as a few hard-boiled eggs, jars of potted meat and cucumber sandwiches. The books evoke thoughts of splendid picnics under sunny blue skies, washed down with ginger beer and home-made lemonade.

As Dr Joan Ransley, honorary lecturer in human nutrition at the University of Leeds, notes:

'The food eaten in the books anchors the Famous Five to a definite period in dietary history. During and immediately after the Second World War British children ate well but austerely and Blyton is true to this.' In other words, they ate healthily but not heartily. Well over half of the books were written during food rationing.

Perhaps Blyton is consciously enticing her readers with elaborate descriptions of foods way beyond the ration book allowance.

In *Five On a Treasure Island*, a simple spread of cold ham, salad, bacon and eggs, plums and a ginger cake fuelled the discovery of gold ingots on Kirrin Island. But over the years, as the Five go off in a caravan, or camping on Billycock Hill, the author has discovered the importance of food in recounting a good yarn:

'A large ham sat on the table, and there were crusty loaves of new bread. Crisp lettuces, dewy and cool, and red radishes were side by side in a big glass dish, great slabs of butter and jugs of creamy milk'

– simple descriptive skills which make the food hugely appealing.

Staples are found throughout: ham, bacon, eggs, the ubiquitous ginger beer and lemonade, together with loaves of crusty bread and cakes and buns. But luxuries – chocolate, for example – don't find their way onto the menu until the postwar years. Blyton doesn't goad us with unobtainable 'exotics' as Elizabeth David did in the 1950s, rather she describes familiar foodstuffs, albeit available to her readers in much

The children manage a structured approach to eating. Breakfast, lunch, dinner and supper all mark out the day. Even while cavorting across the moors in search of spook trains, the Five will stop and sit down so that a meal becomes an enjoyable social interaction. Mealtimes provide an opportunity for the children to share thoughts and to take in all that is happening to them. In today's climate of economic uncertainty, we could do worse than adopt Blyton's approach to eating and take the time to enjoy simple foods.

reduced quantities through the rationing system.

The Five eat a balanced diet. Despite an abundance of humbugs, toffees and ginger pop, when grouped into the five main food categories (fruit and vegetable; meat and fish; dairy; starchy foods; high fat/sugar foods), no one group outweighs another. This comes naturally to the children rather than by diktat. Sweets are eaten sparingly; hunks of crusty bread are accompanied by handfuls of radishes or fresh fruit.

BEHIND THE SCENES . . .

These days, most book manuscripts are produced digitally but computers weren't available when Enid Blyton wrote her Famous Five books …

Very little survives of Enid Blyton's archives, but on these pages you can see some of her manuscripts for the Famous Five stories (as well as some of the many hand-written diaries she kept). Enid wrote straight onto a manual typewriter, using two fingers. She didn't enjoy learning to type, but was persuaded by her first husband, Hugh, in 1927. It seemed to slow her down at first but after a couple of months of dedicated practice, she could type as fast as she could write in longhand. By the end of that year she was able to boast that she'd typed 6,000 words in a day!

FIVE HAVE A
WONDERFUL
TIME

by
·ENID BLYTON

Illustrated by Eileen Soper

London HODDER & STOUGHTON Limited

THIS IS THE ORIGINAL TYPESCRIPT OF

FIVE GO TO MYSTERY MOOR

which is the 13ᵗʰ and latest of the "Famous Five" books.

I do not write my books by hand, but type them straight out of my head. You will see the corrections I have made before sending the book to the publisher.

I

Five Have Plenty of Fun.

Chapter I. At Kirrin Again. ?

"I feel as if we've been at Kirrin for about
a month already!" said Anne, stretching herself out on the
warm sand, and digging her toes in. "And we've only just come."

"Yes - it's funny how we settle down at Kirrin
so quickly," said Dick. "We only came yesterday, and I agree
with you, Anne - it seems as if we've been here ages. I love
Kirrin."

"I hope this weather lasts out the three
weeks we've got left of the holiday," said Julian, rolling
away from Timmy, who was pawing at him, trying to make him
play. "Go away, Timmy. You're too energetic. We've bathed, had
a run, played ball - and that's quite enough for a little
while. Go and play with the crabs."

"Woof!" said Timmy, disgusted. Then he
pricked up his ears as he heard a tinkling noise from the prom-
enade. He barked again.

"Trust old Timmy to hear the ice-cream
man," said Dick. "Anyone want an ice-cream?"

Everyone did, so Anne collected the money

This is the original typescript
of
FIVE HAVE PLENTY OF FUN

(one of the books in the
"Famous Five" series.

Foreword.

Dear Children, (especially Famous Five Club Members,)

This is the thirteenth adventure that the Famous
Five have had. The same characters appear in it - Julian,
Dick, George, Anne - and Timmy the dog, and it is, of
course, quite complete in itself.

First I meant to write six of these Famous Five
books for you. But when I came to six, you said "No-
you must go on!" So I said I would do another six and
make it twelve. But when I had finished the twelfth,
in came thousands of letters again, "But you CAN'T stop
at twelve. Please go on forever!" So here is the
thirteenth for you, and I hope you will like it as much
as you like the others.

The names of the other books are-:

FIVE ON A TREASURE ISLAND
FIVE GO ADVENTURING AGAIN
FIVE RUN AWAY TOGETHER
FIVE GO TO SMUGGLER'S TOP
FIVE GO OFF IN A CARAVAN
FIVE ON KIRRIN ISLAND AGAIN
FIVE GO OFF TO CAMP
FIVE GET INTO TROUBLE
FIVE FALL INTO ADVENTURE
FIVE ON A HIKE TOGETHER
FIVE HAVE A WONDERFUL TIME
FIVE GO DOWN TO THE SEA

One more thing. The lovers of the Famous Five
books have formed a club, called the Famous Five Club.
For particulars of this, see the page at the end of
the book.

My love to you all

From

Enid Blyton.

SUNNY STORIES AND ENID BLYTON'S MAGAZINE

In 1922 Enid started contributing short stories and poems to the weekly paper, *Teachers World*. A year later she was given her own column, 'From My Window', which was replaced by a weekly letter in 1927. In 1929 she was given her own 'Children's Page' which had stories, poems and weekly letters from both Enid and her fox-terrier Bobs.

In 1927 she was asked by George Newnes to provide two booklets a month for a new series, *Sunny Stories for Little Folks*. Some of these had one story divided into chapters, whilst others had three or four short stories. All issues were available to buy in newsagents for several months after publication. After 250 of these, Newnes decided in 1937 to relaunch *Sunny Stories* as a weekly magazine. From this point Enid started

serialising full-length novels which were later released as books. She also started writing short stories using characters such as Amelia Jane, Mister Meddle, Mr Twiddle and others, who were to appear on a regular basis until Enid left *Sunny Stories* in 1953 after 553 issues. A month or so later she launched *Enid Blyton's Magazine* which eventually closed in 1959 after 162 issues.

Five Go Off to Camp was the only Famous Five story to be serialised in *Sunny Stories*, but a further four were used in her magazine, *Five Go Down to the Sea*, *Five On a Secret Trail*, *Five Go to Billycock Hill* and *Five Get Into a Fix*. After the closure of her magazine, a further three books were serialised in *Princess*, a new weekly magazine for girls, *Five at Finniston Farm*, *Five Go to Demon's Rocks* and *Five Together Again*, although two of these had slightly different titles when the books were published.

Eileen Soper produced original illustrations for the magazines which were not used in the books.

BET YOU DIDN'T KNOW . . .

Enid Blyton's Magazine

- A particular formation of five planes in the Red Arrows is nicknamed 'Enid', after Enid Blyton's Famous Five.

- Enid Blyton intended the sixth book, *Five On Kirrin Island Again*, to be the last book in the series. On the back cover of the first edition of the seventh title, *Five Go Off to Camp*, the blurb said, 'The series that was meant to end at the sixth book and hasn't. The children would not allow it and Enid Blyton is glad.'

- And then, in *Five Go to Mystery Moor*, Enid wrote, 'First I meant to write six of these Famous Five books for you. But when I came to six, you said, "No – you must go on!" So I said I would do another six and make it twelve. But when I finished the twelfth, in came thousands of letters again. "But you can't stop at twelve. Please go on forever!" So here is the thirteenth for you.'

- When *Five On a Treasure Island* was produced as an eight-episode television serial in 1957, Enid auditioned the children who played Julian, George, Dick and Anne.

- In 1957, *Five On a Treasure Island* was produced for the Saturday morning Children's Film Foundation serial which was screened in cinemas. Enid was involved with the production of the eight sixteen-minute episodes – and she may even have cast the children who played Julian, George, Dick and Anne.

- When Enid Blyton launched her Magazine in March 1953, the first book to be serialised was *Five Go Down to the Sea*. Enid wrote, 'You begged me for an exciting, mysterious "Five" tale with fun and laughter in it, and so I have written it for you'. Eileen Soper did a wonderful cover for a mock up of the magazine which was sadly never used anywhere – but you can see it on this page.

- In the book *Secret Seven Win Through*, Colin brings his set of Famous Five books to the cave where the Secret Seven are holding their society meetings.

- Enid Blyton could write a whole Famous Five book in only four and a half days. She once said to her literary agent, George Greenfield, 'I'm going to start a new Famous Five on Monday and I have to finish by lunch on Friday, as Kenneth wants to play golf that afternoon.' (Kenneth was Enid Blyton's husband.)

- In 1989, the Renault motor company decided to discontinue their popular 5 model and to farewell it with a bang, they launched the Famous Five Renault (with special features including a glass sunroof, tinted windows, special wheel-trims and Famous Five decals). Only 1,600 cars were released in this livery.

NAME SQUARE

Examine the square shown here and see if you can find the mystery words hidden inside. Start at the top left hand corner and move one letter at a time in any direction except diagonally. Each name starts in a square next to the last letter of the previous word and all letters are used once.

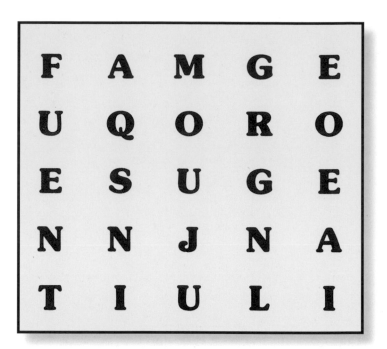

F	A	M	G	E
U	Q	O	R	O
E	S	U	G	E
N	N	J	N	A
T	I	U	L	I

SPOT THE DIFFERENCE!

Here are two versions of the original hardback cover for *Five On Kirrin Island Again*. Apart from the variance in colour – which can still happen today when books are reprinted – can you spot the main difference between the images? Nobody caught it first time round – but it was corrected for a later reprint!

FIVE HAVE A PUZZLING TIME

As well as the twenty-one novels, Enid Blyton wrote eight short stories about the Five, which were wonderful adventures and mysteries in themselves. Here is a taster of one of them. You'll want to read on for sure!

It was dark and very quiet in Kirrin Cottage – almost midnight. The Five were all in bed – yes, Timmy, the dog, too, for he was lying on George's feet, his usual place at night. He wasn't having a very comfortable time, because George, whose real name was Georgina, was so restless.

She tossed and turned and groaned – and at last awoke Anne, who was in the bed next to her.

'What's the matter, George?' said Anne, sleepily. 'Is your tooth aching again?'

'Yes, it's awful,' said George, sitting up with her hand to her cheek. 'Get off my feet, Timmy, I'll just *have* to get up and walk about!'

'Poor George,' said Anne. 'Good thing you're going to the dentist tomorrow!'

'Don't remind me of that!' said George, walking up and down the bedroom. 'Go to sleep, Anne – I didn't mean to disturb you.'

The big clock in the hall downstairs struck twelve, very slowly and solemnly. Anne listened, then her eyes shut and she fell asleep again. George went to the window and looked out over Kirrin Bay, holding a hand to her painful cheek. Timmy jumped off the bed and stood beside her, paws on the windowsill. He knew that George was in pain, and he was troubled. He rested his head against her hand and gave it a tiny lick.

'Dear Timmy,' said George. 'I hope *you'll* never have toothache! You'd go mad! Look at Kirrin Bay – isn't it lovely? And you can just see Kirrin Island – *my* island, Timmy – looming up in the darkness!'

Suddenly George stiffened and frowned. She stared across the bay, and then turned and called urgently to Anne.

'Anne! Quick, wake up! *Anne!* Come and see! There's a light shining out on Kirrin Island, a light, I tell you! Somebody's there – on *my* island! Anne, come and see!'

Anne sat up sleepily. 'What's the matter, George? What did you say?'

'I said there's a light on Kirrin Island!

Somebody must be there – without permission too! I'll get my boat and row out right now!'

George was very angry indeed, and Timmy gave a little growl. He would most certainly deal with whoever it was on the island!

'Oh, George – don't be an idiot!' said Anne. 'As if you could get your boat and row across the bay in the middle of the night! You must be mistaken!' She jumped out of bed and went to the window. 'Where's this light?'

'It's gone – it went out just as you jumped out of bed,' said George. 'Who can be there, Anne? I'll wake the boys and tell them. We'll get my boat.'

She went quickly down to the room where Dick and Julian lay asleep and shook them roughly.

'Wake up! Oh, PLEASE wake up!

Something's going on over at Kirrin Island. I saw a light there. WAKE UP, Julian.'

George's excited voice not only woke up the boys, but her father as well. He sat up in bed in the next room, thinking there must be burglars in the house!

'Robbers, my dear!' he hissed in his wife's ear, making her start up in fright. 'Where's my big stick?'

'Quentin, it's only the children!' said his wife, sleepily. 'I expect George's toothache is worse. I'll go and see.'

Everybody met in the boys' room. 'What on earth is all this about?' demanded George's father.

'There's a light on Kirrin Island,' said George, quite fiercely. 'On *my* island! I'm going to see who it is – and so is Timmy. If no one will come with me I'll go alone.'

'Indeed you won't go,' said her father, raising his voice angrily. 'Get back to bed! Rowing to Kirrin Island in the middle of the night! You must be mad. There *can't* be anyone there. You've had a bad dream, or something.'

'Dad, there's a *light* there – I saw it!' said George, in a voice as loud as her father's. He went at once to the window and looked out. 'Rubbish!' he said. 'Not a glimmer of any sort to be seen! You dreamt it!'

'I did NOT!' said George, angrily. 'Somebody is there, I tell you. Trespassing!'

'Well, *let* them trespass!' said her father. 'You can go over tomorrow.'

'I *can't*!' almost wailed George. 'I've got to

go to the dentist, and have this nasty, horrible, awful tooth out. I *must* go tonight!'

'Shut up, George,' said Julian. 'Be sensible. Whoever's there will still be there tomorrow. I'll go over with Dick. Anyway, there's no light there now – you probably made a mistake. Go to bed, for goodness' sake.'

George flung out of the boys' room, and went to her own, furious. Timmy went with her, licking her now and again. Why couldn't he and George go off together, this very minute? Timmy was quite ready to!

'Now my tooth's aching worse than ever!' said poor George, angry and miserable, dumping herself violently on her bed. Her mother came over to her with a glass of water and two small pills.

'Take these, George,' she said. 'Your tooth will soon stop aching. Please be sensible, dear.'

'That's one thing George can't be!' said Anne, 'Cheer up, George – that tooth will be gone tomorrow – and there won't be anyone on your island, you'll see – and everything will be right again'.

George grunted, and lay down with her aching cheek on her hand. She meant to slip out of bed, and go down to her boat as soon as the house was quiet again. But the little pills quickly did their work, and in five minutes her tooth had stopped aching, and she was fast asleep.

In the morning when she awoke, she remembered at once what she had seen the night before – a light on her island! And then she remembered the dentist – oh dear, two horrible thoughts – someone trespassing on her precious island – and a tooth to come out! She sat up in bed.

'Anne! My tooth has stopped aching. I won't go to the dentist, I'll go to Kirrin Island with Timmy and the boys.'

But her father thought differently, and after a really furious battle between the hot-tempered George and her equally hot-tempered father, George was packed off with her mother in the car, for her visit to the dentist! Timmy went with her, quite alarmed at all the goings-on!

'Poor George,' said Anne, as the car went off down the road. 'She does get so worked up about things.'

'Well, anyone gets upset with toothache,' said Julian. He stared out over Kirrin Bay, which was as blue as cornflowers that morning. 'I wonder if George *did* see a light on the island last night? *You* didn't see one, did you, Anne, when you awoke?'

'No. It was all dark there,' said Anne. 'Honestly, I think George must have dreamt it! Anyway she can take out her boat this afternoon, and we'll go with her, and have a good look round – that should satisfy her!'

'She may not feel like doing anything except having a bit of a rest,' said Dick. 'She's had toothache for days now, and it does get you down. I tell you what – we three will get the boat and go over to the island this morning – then, when we find nothing and nobody there – except the rabbits and the jackdaws – we can tell George, and she won't worry any more!'

'Right!' said Julian. 'Let's go now, straight away! Uncle Quentin will be glad to be rid of us – he's working hard this morning on one of his newest problems.'

George's father was glad to hear that the three were going off for the morning.

'Now I'll have the house to myself,' he said, thankfully. 'Except for Joanna, of course. I hope she doesn't take it into her head to clean out the boiler this morning – I MUST have peace and quiet.'

'You ought to invent a boiler that cleans *itself* out with hardly a whisper!' said Anne, smiling at her uncle. 'Anyway, we'll be out of your way. We're just going!'

They went to the beach, to get George's boat. There it was, ready waiting! Julian looked across to where Kirrin Island lay peacefully in the sun. He was quite certain there was nobody there! George must have dreamt the light she had seen shining in the night.

'We'll row right round the island and see if there's a boat tied up anywhere, or beached,' said Dick, taking the oars. 'If there isn't, we'll know there's no one there. It's too far for anyone to swim to. Well – here we go!'

And away they went in the warm spring sunshine, the little waves lapping cheerfully round the boat.

Anne leaned back and let her hand dabble in the water – what fun to go over to the island and see all the rabbits – there would be young ones there too, now.

'Here we are, almost at the island,' said Julian. 'In and out of the rocks we go! I'm sorry for anyone who tries to come here in the middle of the night, unable to see what rocks to avoid! Not a sign of a boat anywhere – George *must* have dreamt it all!'

Dick rowed the boat carefully between the rocks that guarded the island.

'We'll land at our usual little cove,' he said. 'I bet no one else would know how to get there if they didn't already know the way!'

A low wall of sharp rocks came into sight and Dick rounded it neatly. Now they could see the cove where they meant to land – a little natural harbour, with a calm inlet of water running up to a smooth stretch of sand.

'The water's like glass here,' said Anne. 'I can see the bottom of the cove.' She leapt out and helped the boys to pull in the boat.

'*Look* at the rabbits!' said Dick, as they walked up the smooth sandy beach. 'Tame as ever!'

A small baby rabbit came lolloping up to Anne. 'You sweet little thing!' she said, trying to pick it up. 'You're just like a toy bunny!' But the tiny creature lolloped away again.

'Good thing Timmy's not here,' said Julian. 'He always looks so miserable when he sees the rabbits, because he knows he mustn't chase them!'

They came to the old ruined castle that had been built long ago on the island. The ancient, broken-down entrance led into a great yard, overgrown with weeds. Now the jackdaws came down from the tower, and chacked loudly round them in a very friendly manner. Some of them flew down to the children's feet, and walked about as tame as hens in a farm yard.

'Well – it doesn't look as if anyone's here,' said Julian, staring round and about.

'And there was no boat anywhere,' said Anne. 'So how could anyone have come here? Let's see if there are any signs of a fire having been lighted. The flames would be seen at night, if so.'

They began to hunt all around. They went in and out of the old castle, examining the floor – but there was no sign of anyone having made a fire.

'If George saw a light, then there must be a lamp or lantern somewhere,' said Dick. 'Anne, did she see the light high up on the island – as if it came from the tower?'

'She didn't say,' said Anne. 'But I should *think* it must have been high up. We'll go up the old broken-down tower steps as far as we can, shall we? We might see something there – perhaps a lantern. It's possible, I suppose, that someone might have been signalling for some reason!'

But, no matter how they searched, the three could find nothing to explain the light that George had said she saw.

'Let's go and lie down on the grass, and watch the rabbits,' said Anne. 'Hey – why did the jackdaws all fly up then – and why are they chacking so much? What frightened them?'

'Funny!' said Julian, staring at the big black birds, circling round and round above them, calling 'chack-chack-chack' so excitedly. '*We* didn't scare them, I'm sure. I suppose there *can't* be someone else here?'

'Well – we'll walk round the island and examine the rocks sticking up here and there,'

said Dick, puzzled about the jackdaws, too. 'Someone might be hiding behind one of them.'

'I'm going to take off my sandals,' said Anne. 'I love running on the smooth sand in bare feet. I'll have a paddle, too – the water's quite warm today!'

The boys wandered off round the island. Anne sat down and undid her sandals. She set them by a big stone, so that she could easily find them again, and ran down to the sea. Little waves were splashing over the smooth golden sand, and Anne ran into them, curling up her toes in pleasure.

'It's really almost warm enough to swim,' she thought. 'What a lovely little island this is – and how lucky George is to own it. I wish *I* had an island belonging to my family, that I could call my own. If I had, I suppose I'd worry, too, like George, if I thought anyone was trespassing here – scaring the rabbits – and even perhaps snaring them!'

Soon Julian and Dick came back together, having gone all round the island, and looked into every cranny. They called to Anne.

'Hello, paddler! Is the water nice and warm? We should have brought our swimming things.'

'We haven't seen a sign of a single soul,' said Dick. 'Better go home again. George may be back by now – wanting to tell us about her tooth, and what she's been through. Poor George!'

'I'll put on my sandals,' said Anne, drying her feet by scrabbling them in the warm sand. She

ran to the big stone by which she had put them. She stopped – and stared in surprise.

'What's happened to one of my sandals? Dick – Ju – have you taken one? Where have you put it?'

'Sandals? No – we didn't even know where you'd put them,' said Julian. 'There's one of them there, look – the other must be somewhere near.'

But it wasn't. No matter how they all looked, only one of Anne's sandals could be found!

'*Well*! How silly!' said Anne, amazed. 'I *know* I put them both together, just here. I know I did! Anyway, there's no one to take one of my sandals – and even if there were, why take one, and not both?'

'Perhaps a rabbit took one?' suggested Dick, with a grin. 'Or a jackdaw – they're really mischievous birds, you know!'

'A jackdaw surely couldn't pick up a *sandal*!' said Anne. 'It'd be too heavy. And I can't *imagine* a rabbit running off with one!'

'Well – it's not there,' said Dick, thinking to himself that Anne must have been mistaken about putting them both by the big stone. He hunted round, but could not see the other one anywhere – strange! However – there certainly was no one on the island – and, if there had been, someone wouldn't have been so silly as to risk being discovered by stealing one little sandal, in full view of Anne!

'We'll have to leave your sandal, wherever it is, Anne,' said Julian, at last. 'We ought to get back. Well – the only thing we can tell George is that we saw no one at all here – but that one sandal mysteriously disappeared!'

'Oh no!' said Anne, not bothering to put on her one sandal. 'Now I'll have to spend some of my precious pocket money to buy a pair of new sandals. How annoying!'

THE FIENDISH FAMOUS FIVE QUIZ

Are you ready to test your knowledge of the Famous Five? Here's a test to challenge even the most dedicated fans. The answers are on page 64. No peeking!

1. What is the name of Uncle Quentin's wife? She is also George's mother.

2. Name the two artists staying at Kirrin Farmhouse in *Five Go Adventuring Again*.

3. In the first book, who looked after Timothy for George when she was not allowed to keep him at Kirrin Cottage?

4. Name the cook who arrives at Kirrin Cottage just before the Famous Five have their second adventure.

5. What is the name of the housemistress at the girls' school? (She is mentioned in *Five On a Hike Together*)

6. What sort of animals does Mr Slither have in his fairground act? (See *Five Have a Wonderful Time*)

7. What are the names of the twins the Five meet excavating the old Roman camp on Kirrin Common in *Five On a Secret Trail*?

8. In *Five Go to Mystery Moor*, what is the name of the tomboy the Five meet at Captain Johnson's Riding School?

9. Julian spots some niches in the side of the hole that leads to one of the secret passages at Smuggler's Top. What are these niches and what are they used for? (See *Five Go to Smuggler's Top*)

10. In *Five On Kirrin Island Again*, Dick says that scientists are VIPs. What do the letters VIP stand for?

11. When the villains are moving stone slabs in the ruined cottage on Kirrin Common they use a jemmy. What sort of tool is that? (See *Five On a Secret Trail*)

12. What name does Pierre Lenoir give to the network of passages that honeycomb Castaway Hill in *Five Go to Smuggler's Top*?

13. In the eleventh mystery, who discovers the entrance to the secret passage that runs through the walls of Faynights Castle?

14. One entrance to the secret passage on Kirrin Common is found close to the spring of fresh water. Where does the passage lead?

15. Which red-headed villain had his headquarters on the clifftop at Port Limmersley in *Five Fall Into Adventure*?

16. While on the moor at night in *Five On a Hike Together*, Dick and Anne hear bells ringing. They later learn that this is a signal from the prison on the moor. What does the signal mean?

17. What was once quarried on Mystery Moor?

18. In book seven, how does George try to find out when the boys are leaving their tent to go and look for Spook Trains in the middle of the night?

19. How does Richard Kent escape from Owl's Dene in *Five Get Into Trouble*?

20. When the Five are exploring the secret passage at Faynights Castle they find something on the floor that shows them other people have been along the passage recently. What is it they find? (See *Five Have a Wonderful Time*)

21. In the twelfth book in the series, what clues do the Five find in the Wreckers' Tower that leads them to believe that someone has been there with an oil lamp?

22. In *Five Go Down to the Sea*, who unlocks the door after the Five have been locked into the storeroom they discover along the secret passage from the Wreckers' Tower?

23. How does Julian prevent the villains escaping from the undergound cave on the site of the old Roman camp on Kirrin Cottage? (See *Five On a Secret Trail*)

24. What are the names of the ponies who pull the caravans in *Five Go Off in a Caravan*?

25. What does Timmy get in his foot while on Mystery Moor in the book which features that location in its title?

GUESS WHO?

The Famous Five have lots in common – and their shared adventures bring them closer together. But they each have qualities which are uniquely their own. Which character does each of the statements below most closely describe? (There is more than one attribute for each member of the gang!)

1. **Wishes she were a boy.**

2. **Expert at guarding the Five.**

3. **Tendency to be over-protective.**

4. **Used to be a cry-baby when young.**

5. **The natural leader.**

6. **Excellent at games.**

7. **Particularly fond of ice-cream (but not ginger beer).**

8. **Enjoys wearing pretty dresses.**

9. **The oldest member of the Five.**

10. **Hot-tempered.**

11. **Loves to have a laugh.**

12. **Very good at handling adult situations.**

The answers are on page 64.

Julian

Dick

Anne

George

Timmy

ANIMALS IN THE FAMOUS FIVE

We all know that Timmy is the most important animal in the Famous Five adventures but Enid Blyton created other interesting animals for the stories. You can meet them in this section. The number in brackets refers to the book where the animals feature.

Timmy

Barker and Growler (5): Nobby's two trained dogs. They are clever, well-behaved terriers that can perform a number of tricks. They can dribble a football around with their noses and walk on their hind legs. Barker nearly dies after eating poisoned meat left out for Timmy by Tiger Dan.

Beauty (11): One of the two pythons owned by Mr Slither at the time he and other fair folk are camping at Faynights Field. Beauty likes being handled and enjoys being polished by his master to get rid of mites that lodge themselves under his scales. Beauty likes nothing better than to curl round a friend, though as Mr Slither points out, it is important not to let him get a good grip with the end of his tail, otherwise the result could be fatal! **Jo** is very fond of Beauty and takes him with her when she tries to rescue the Five from **Faynights Castle.** Beauty plays a very important part at the end of the adventure

when he scares **Jeffrey Pottersham** and his friends and forces them to retreat into a room where Jo bolts them in.

Biddy (7): The four year old collie belonging to **Jock**. Biddy lives on Olly's farm and has just had four puppies.

Binky (16): The collie dog owned by **Toby Thomas** of Billycock Farm who enjoys shaking paws with everyone he meets – including Timmy. Binky has 'bright brown eyes.'

Charlie the Chimp (21): The brown eyed chimpanzee owned by **Mr Wooh** at Tapper's Circus where his skill at playing

Pongo

cricket amazes audiences. Like **Pongo**, the chimp encountered by the Five in *Five Go Off in a Caravan,* Charlie enjoys human company and is ready and willing to help with chores. He is 'as strong as ten men' and happily carries the children's tents etc. when they are camping close to the circus camp. The chimp is very fond of **Mischief, Tinker's** little pet monkey. Charlie loves sweets and bananas and opens the bolt on his cage door himself when he wants to go for a walk!

Chippy (see the short story collection): A tiny brown monkey with a comical face owned by **Bobby Loman**. The Five first see Chippy up a tree clutching a stolen barley sugar.

Chummy (see the short story collection): A large cross-bred Alsatian dog owned by **Bobby Loman.** After his grandfather threatens to have the dog put to sleep for biting a person, Bobby, Chummy and **Chippy**, his pet monkey, run away to Kirrin Island where the Five discover them in hiding.

Clip (13): A small skewball horse owned by **Sniffer's father.** The pony is overworked and under-fed. When he goes lame he is brought to **Captain Johnson** at his riding school for treatment. After a rest in the stable Clip is able to resume work pulling **Sniffer's** caravan.

Clopper (12): Not a real animal at all but a canvas pantomime horse operated by two men. Clopper is the most popular act at the the Barnies travelling shows. His head is beautifully modelled with eyes that can open, close and swivel. His mouth too can be opened and closed to reveal large teeth. His skilled operators can make him

march, tap-dance, jump like a kangaroo and sit down crossed legged. Inside his head is a secret compartment where the **Guv'nor** conceals smuggled drugs.

Curly (16): The piglet owned by **Benny Thomas** at Billycock Farm, and so named because of his curly tail. Curly takes an active part in the rescue of **Jeff Thomas** and Ray Wells after falling into the cave in which the pair are being kept prisoner. Curly carries a message back to Billycock Farm chalked in black chalk on his back!

Curly

Dai, Bob, Tang, Doon, Joll, Rafe and Hal (17): The seven dogs belonging to **Morgan Jones** of Magga Glen Farm. Although these dogs do not endear themselves to George after three of them attack Timmy, they more than make up for the little nip they gave him when they help Morgan to save **Aily,** her father and the Five after they are captured by **Llewellyn Thomas** and his miners while exploring the underground passages and river that runs through **Old Towers Hill.**

Dobby (5): The horse owned by Julian's family that was once used to pull the pony cart. When not being borrowed by friends, Dobby spends most of his time in a field close to the children's home. In *Five Go Off in a Caravan* he is used to pull one of the two small caravans used by the Five.

Fany (17): The little lamb belonging to **Aily**. It is because Fany frisks off down the tunnel next to the underground river under Old Towers Hill that the Five and Fany are caught by the miners working there.

Blinky

Growler (5): See Barker and Growler.

Jet (short for Jet Propelled) (15): The lively little black and white mongrel owned by **Guy Lawdler**. It has a 'ridiculously long tail' which is always on the wag. The animal is blind in one eye but his other eye is exceedingly bright. As with other small dogs the Five meet, Timmy got on well with Jet.

Liz (13): One of the strangest looking dogs that the ever Five meet is Liz, the ex-circus dog owned by **Sniffer**. Liz is part spaniel, part poodle with odd bits of something else. When the children see her they think she looks like a hearthrug, and Timmy can't make her out at all, particularly when she walks up to him on her back legs and starts to perform forward rolls in front of him. The two dogs become very good friends.

Mischief (19/21): The small, brown-eyed monkey owned by **Tinker Hayling**. Despite being full of mischief it is almost impossible to dislike the little creature. **Joan**, the cook, is particularly fond of the monkey and gives him tit-bits. At first Timmy is wary of the little creature – particularly after it takes his bone – but when Mischief offers Timmy a biscuit as a peace offering the two become firm friends, with Mischief curling up between Timmy's front legs to sleep. Mischief finds a gold coin that helps the Five to discover the whereabouts of the 'Wreckers' hoard of treasure at Demon's Rocks. When Tapper's Circus comes to **Big Hollow House**, Mischief becomes good friends with **Charlie the Chimp.**

Nosey (18): The tame jackdaw at **Finniston Farm** owned by **Henry and Harriet Philpot**. The bird has been a pet of the twins since they nursed it back to health after falling down a chimney and breaking its wing. Like most jackdaws Nosey is attracted to bright objects and early on in the story tries to steal Dick's watch. Later Nosey, together with **Snippet** the dog, discovers the course of the passage that runs between the site of **Finniston Castle** and the old chapel.

Old Lady (6): The elephant at Mr Georgio's Circus who likes bathing in the lake and squirting water over anyone who comes close.

Pongo (5): The mischievous chimpanzee at Mr Gorgio's circus amuses the children with his antics but is extremely strong and can be fierce if he sees anyone he cares for being hurt. Pongo is a great mimic and will copy the actions of those around him. He gets on well with Timmy but will insist on trying to shake hands with the dog's tail instead of his paw! He can be a bit of a pick-pocket and is particularly fond of anything that he can eat, though he is rather surprised when a sweet sticks his teeth together. He enjoys ginger beer almost as much as the children and is given his own bottle when they have a picnic. If told off for naughty behaviour he covers his face with his paw but peeps through his fingers. He is a great help in protecting the children from **Tiger Dan** and **Lou** in *Five Go Off in a Caravan*. He is knocked out by a large stone thrown at him by Tiger Dan but by the end of the adventure has managed to get his revenge.

Sally (14): The tiny black poodle owned by **Berta Wright** has a sharp little nose quick eyes and slim legs. Her woolly fur is cut into a 'fashionable look'. Despite being much smaller than Timmy, Sally has sharp teeth and Berta tells the children that if provoked Sally can make a good impression on somebody's leg with them! As with other dogs they meet, Timmy gets on well with Sally.

Snippet (18): The tiny black poodle owned by **Henry and Harriet Philpot** of **Finniston Farm**. Snippet, together with **Nosey**, the jackdaw, discovers a way into the tunnel that runs from the site of **Finniston Castle** to the old chapel.

Tinker (3): The dog belonging to **the Stick family** has a dirty white coat and is rather mangy and moth eaten to look at. He is re-named 'Stinker' by the Five. He usually has his tail down between his legs and is terrified of Timothy who chases him as if he were a rabbit!

Trotter (5): The milkman's sturdy black horse borrowed by the Five to pull the girl's caravan in *Five Go Off in a Caravan*. He gets on not only with **Dobby**, but is also very fond of Timmy. His comical antics amuse the children, particularly when he tries to snuggle under one of the caravans with Timmy!

WRITING THE FAMOUS FIVE

A personal account by Enid Blyton's daughter, Gillian Baverstock

Enid Blyton taught herself to type in 1926. She typed faster than most typists, even though she used just two fingers. She said she could easily write 10–12,000 words a day and the reason she did not write more was because her arms became tired.

This helps to explain why it took Enid Blyton only four to five days to write a Famous Five book of approximately 40,000 words in length. When she started the first in the series, *Five On a Treasure Island*, she knew only what type of book she had to write and its length. She put her typewriter on her knees, closed her eyes and waited for the story to come into her imagination.

After a few minutes she saw four children – and soon knew their names and relationships. She was pleased when Timmy appeared because she knew her readers liked animals in their stories.

Gradually the setting grew in her imagination.

Kirrin Cottage, the sea and a rowing boat, and island with a castle on the top. She heard the children talking and playing in her head and saw George scowling at the others.

The ideas kept surging up from her imagination and she found it hard to keep up on her typewriter. She said it was like watching a film inside her head and she did not know what was going to happen until she started to write what she saw.

She kept to a daily timetable while writing a book, starting at ten o'clock and stopping for lunch at one o'clock. She would start again about a quarter to two and finish writing for the day at about half past four. She didn't really like noise and interruptions but when I came home from school I would run in to say 'hello' and grab the pages she had written that day. I read them in my bedroom and at tea-time I would beg her to tell me what happened next, but she never would and I would have to wait until the next day.

She had far more to do in a day than just writing. She read over what she had written that day and corrected any proofs of other books that her publishers had sent her. She would check artists' pictures carefully, then carefully pack the pictures up again – and there was no Sellotape in those days, only sealing wax. Then she would have to answer all her letters – at least fifty every day; some business letters and some from children. She answered them all and never used a secretary.

She was the busiest person I have ever known, yet she still had time to read, to talk, to arrange her flowers, to play golf or tennis, or to garden. However, when she was writing a long book she had little time for anything else but she did not mind because, for her, writing was not work – it was pleasure.

Gillian was Enid Blyton's elder daughter.
She was born in 1931 and died in 2007.

ANOTHER MYSTERY AT MYSTERY MOOR

The column on the left below contains words from the chapter titles of *Five Go to Mystery Moor*. Can you unscramble them? We've included the chapter number to help you. Write the unscrambled words in the spaces in the column on the right. If you put all the circled letters together, they'll tell you the first part of the message that Timmy carried back to Henry.

12	**A W A R I L Y**	_ _ _ _ (O) _ _
5	**C H E E D H A A**	_ (O) _ _ _ _ _ _
4	**B L E A T S**	_ _ (O) _ _ _
2	**H Y E N R**	_ _ _ (O) _
13	**S O N E I**	_ _ _ _ (O)
14	**D A L P E S E**	(O) _ _ _ _ _ _
16	**R I B L E T R E**	_ _ (O) _ _ _ _ _
20	**G I R N O M N**	_ _ _ _ (O) _ _
10	**S T R I P A N**	_ _ _ _ _ _ (O)
19	**O D O G**	_ (O) _ _
13	**G H I T N**	(O) _ _ _ _
7	**R E G G E O**	_ _ _ _ _ (O)
15	**G L I N T S T A R**	_ _ _ (O) _ _ _ _ _
21	**Y S T E R M Y**	_ _ (O) _ _ _ _

What did the message say?

Do you know who wrote it?

FIVE GO TO SMUGGLER'S TOP

The Famous Five are staying at Smuggler's Top with the Lenoir family. Sooty Lenoir tells them his stepfather is full of secrets and says strange things happen at Smuggler's Top. Mr Lenoir doesn't like dogs much at all. So when they're in Sooty's room and they hear someone coming, they hide Timmy …

'Hello, Block,' said Sooty. 'Block's my stepfather's assistant,' he explained. 'He's been here about a year. Suddenly appeared one day! He's deaf, but he seems to sense what we say,' he added warningly.

'Mr and Mrs Lenoir want to meet your friends,' said Block.

So leaving poor Timmy hidden in the cupboard, Sooty and his sister, Marybelle, took the others downstairs.

Mr Lenoir seemed to be smiling all the time – but he didn't look friendly! He told Sooty he wasn't to take his friends into the catacombs in the hill.

'And I want your promise there'll be no acting about on the city wall and no daredevil climbing,' he added.

Sooty avoided giving his promise. He was grinning as they all left the room …

'I can show you loads of strange places,' he said. 'Winding, secret tunnels in the hills, smugglers' haunts, secret passages …'

Sooty said they could sneak Timmy out from a passage in Marybelle's room. 'We get down it by a rope ladder. The passage comes out at a path near the marshes.'

'Timmy can't climb down a rope ladder!' stormed George. But Marybelle had an idea …

Sooty climbed down first, and Timmy was lowered down to him. Then, one by one, the rest of them followed. Soon they were all standing at the bottom of the hole.

'What about letting him down and getting him up in a big laundry basket with ropes tied round?'

Come on! This is the way out!

As they passed a few more passages, they were unaware of the dark figure peering at them from behind …

'That one leads to Mr Barling's house,' said Sooty. Mr Barling was known as a smuggler.

Soon they came out of a cave-like entrance in the hillside. 'We've got to get that path down there,' said Sooty. 'Be careful you don't slip or you'll land in the marshes!'

They all went down the path, clambering over rocks now and again. Then they climbed over the city wall and into the town. 'Look out! Here's Block,' said Sooty suddenly. 'We'll have to ignore Timmy and if he comes up to any of us, we'll have to pretend to drive him off. Then Block'll think he's a stray!'

Timmy heard his name and jumped up at Sooty. 'Go away, dog!' said Sooty, flapping his arms. Timmy yapped happily. He thought it was a new game.

Then Block came up to them. 'I'll throw a stone at this dog if it's annoying you!' he said. And, to George's horror, Block picked up a big stone.

'How dare you throw stones at a dog!' yelled George, punching Block's arm to make him drop the stone. 'I'll … I'll tell the police!'

'Now, now,' said a voice nearby. 'Pierre, what's the trouble?'

'I'd forgotten Sooty's real name was Pierre!' Anne whispered to Marybelle as Sooty turned to look at the person who'd spoken.

'Oh, Mr Barling,' said Sooty. 'Nothing's the matter, really. This dog keeps following us and Block was going to throw a stone at him. George likes dogs and got angry about it. That's all. No problem!'

Then Mr Barling asked Sooty to introduce him to the others.

'They've come to stay because a tree fell through the roof of their cottage at Kirrin,' Sooty explained.

'Ah, Kirrin, where that clever scientist friends of your stepfather, Pierre, to invite all your friends to stay!'

They all stared at Mr Barling – he'd spoken in such a sneering voice! It was clear he didn't like Mr Lenoir. Well, neither did they, but they didn't like Mr Barling any better!

Mr Barling went on his way and Block had gone into a shop. By now, Timmy was following another dog, so George and the others went after him.

'Wow! That was a narrow escape from Block,' said Julian. 'Bad luck meeting him on our first time out!'

It's all a trifle boring!

When they got back to Smuggler's Top, they had to hide poor Timmy in the cupboard in Sooty's room while they went down for dinner. They felt an uneasy feeling as they waited for Block to serve them.

Later, George led Timmy to the bedroom she was sharing with Anne. It wasn't in the same wing as Sooty's and Maybelle's rooms. 'I hope Block doesn't come out and catch me sneaking Timmy in and out!' said George to Sooty.

George had to sneak Timmy back into Sooty's room early every morning. 'Sneaking Sooty back into Sooty's room every morning is the only exciting thing,' said Julian gloomily. 'Nothing else is happening!'

But a couple of nights later, Sooty shook Julian and Dick awake. 'Come to the box room with me,' he whispered. 'You can see the tower room from there and someone's flashing a light from the window.'

'It isn't my stepfather up there,' said Sooty. 'I heard him snoring as I passed his room. Let's go and see if Block's room is empty.'

'I'll go to the Tower Room and peep through the door!' decided Sooty. 'It's at the top of a twisty staircase. Not much room up there. You two had better wait at the bottom of the stairs.'

Sooty couldn't see into the Tower Room – the keyhole had been blocked up. But he could hear a series of clicks as whoever was in the room kept signalling!

Click, Click...
Click, Click...

The clicking stopped. Someone was walking towards the door! Almost at once the door opened. There was no time for Sooty to run down the stairs …

CREEE-EEEE!

WHAT WILL HAPPEN NEXT? THE COMPLETE VERSION OF THE STORY CONTINUES IN ENID BLYTON'S FULL-LENGTH NOVEL . . .

FIVE GO ADVENTURING AGAIN FIND-A-WORD

Can you find all the words in the list hidden inside the grid? They can run in any direction.

AGAIN	GEORGE	NOISE	SNOW
ARTIST	HUNT	PANEL	STOLEN
AUNT	JOURNEY	PAPERS	SURPRISE
CHILDREN	JULIAN	POLICE	TOGETHER
CHRISTMAS	LESSONS	QUENTIN	TROUBLE
DISCOVERED	LINEN	ROOMS	TUTOR
ENTRANCE	LOCKS	SANDERS	UNPLEASANT
EXCITING	MR ROLAND	SECRET	WALK
FANNY	NIGHT	SHOCK	WILTON

```
M B L N O T L I W P A N E L
T R Y F A N N Y W T O S N I
B E R L Y I T A R T I S T N
C T R O U B L E O O N A B E
L H D C L K A U N T E N U N
Y G R I E A T O J O C D N N
C I B I S S N N S G N E P E
H N H J S C I D N E A R L C
I L Y U O T O T O T R S E I
L R O G N U M V W H T N A L
D B O E S T R A E E N N S O
R L U O Y O T N S R E P A P
E Q O R M R N H E L E B N L
N I A G A S O Y O Y T D T O
N B L E X C I T I N G Y T O
N L O C K S S U R P R I S E
```

The leftover letters spell the name of someone closely connected to *Five Go to Mystery Moor*. Who is it? And how many times does it appear in this puzzle?

Answer: _____

THE FAMOUS FIVE CLUB

In the late summer of 1952, no doubt after receiving scores of pleas in the numerous letters that she received daily, Enid Blyton decided to form a Famous Five Club. This gave her a problem as she had no obvious means of advertising the fact. She was still writing for *Sunny Stories* published by Newnes, who were unwilling to promote a series from another publisher. So she approached Hodder & Stoughton, the Famous Five publishers and asked if they could put a page in the back of the next Famous Five book. This was *Five Have a Wonderful Time*, but the book was already at the printers. They came up with a compromise and produced a bookmark advertising the club, which was tucked into this book and all the reprints of earlier books. They also generously agreed to run the club and to send out badges, membership cards and a printed letter to all new members, and in September 1952 with the publication of the new book, the Famous Five Club was formed. The address of the club, 20 Warwick Square, was that of Hodder & Stoughton. All that was required for membership was a shilling postal order sent to that address.

In March 1953 Enid Blyton left *Sunny Stories* and launched *Enid Blyton's Magazine*, and at last the Club had a proper 'home'. The club had a charitable purpose and all profits were going to the Children's Convalescent Home in Beaconsfield which looked after a maximum of thirty children up to the age of five. News of the Club and the Home was to appear in each issue of the magazine on 'Our News-Sheet', which also carried news of other clubs that Enid ran. After very few issues a 'Famous Five Puzzle Page' was also present in each issue.

The bookmark had clearly done a good job, as in the first issue of her magazine Enid announced that they already had 13,000 members and a cheque for just over £222 had gone to the Home and some new furniture had been ordered. This was the first of many cheques over the years and, perhaps not surprisingly, one of the wards was renamed the Famous Five Ward. Enid named Mr Henry Jones as the man at Hodder & Stoughton who ran the club and told her readers that he not only read all the hundreds of letters that came in, but also sent out all the badges. In August his job became harder still, as from then on Hodder offered three Famous Five books each issue as prizes for one of the puzzles on the 'Famous Five Puzzle Page'.

When *Enid Blyton's Magazine* closed in 1959, there were already 109,000 members. Although this closure meant the loss of the 'headquarters' as Enid had called it, the advertisement for the club continued to appear in all subsequent new editions of all the hardbacks, although the address changed to Arlen House in

(Continued from the other side)

The lovely little badges cost one shilling. Any profit made will go to THE CHILDREN'S CONVALESCENT HOME in Beaconsfield. Send a shilling postal order and an envelope stamped and addressed to yourself inside an envelope addressed to

FAMOUS FIVE CLUB 20 WARWICK SQUARE LONDON E.C.4

You shall have your badge as soon as possible and a letter telling you about the Famous Five Club.

Enid Blyton

THE FAMOUS FIVE CLUB

20 WARWICK SQUARE
LONDON E.C.4

Dear "Famous Five" member,

Well, we have our own "Famous Five" Club at last. Do you like the badge I am sending? It is what hundreds of you suggested to me—just the heads of the Famous Five together.

Now the reason for starting the Club is this; everywhere I go I meet boys and girls who are already my friends because they are friends of the Famous Five. There are hundreds of thousands of you all over the world. The great pity is that I can't recognize you, and you don't recognize each other, which is why, of course, you have begged so often for a badge. And now at last we have one.

If all our members wear their badges we shall know each other at once, and I shall be able to recognize you too; I shall come up to you and speak to you, so look out for me! I shall wear my badge too, of course, so that you will always know me.

Quite a lot of children have suggested a signal of some kind when you see someone else wearing the F.F. badge—such as raising your hand, spreading your five fingers quickly and dropping your hand again. The children who suggested this were thinking that Five Fingers stood for F.F. too. I think I will leave you to think of your own signal, and as

the Club grows we shall see which signal becomes the most popular. It is your Club, and I want you to think out good ideas for it.

Well, that is the first purpose of the Famous Five Club, to recognize each other and show friendliness everywhere. The second purpose is to help children who are not nearly as fortunate as you are.

In the town where I live is a little Home for Children who are ill, or unhappy, or have no father or mother to love them. I am always trying to help these children, and I know you will like to help too. So, whatever money is left over from the shillings paid for your badges is going to this little Home, and will buy happiness for those who have very little of it. I think you know that the Famous Five (yes, Timmy too!) would be the first to help if they could.

Now, you will want to know exactly how many members we have, how much money comes in, how it has been used, and how much we have to give to the Children's Home. So, early in the New Year, please look in our magazine because there I shall tell you all these things. I shall talk about the Club quite a lot, so that everyone will know exactly how it is getting on.

This is only a beginning. We might do all kinds of things with the "Famous Five" Club. Anyway, we will make it a success to start with, and then perhaps we can plan out some more ideas.

Good luck and love from

Enid Blyton

Write the names of your
Club friends below :

....
....
....
....
....
....
....

Paste a photograph
of yourself
here :

Name ....
Address ....
....
....

**THE
Famous Five
Club**

Leicester when Brockhampton took over the publishing in the late 1960s. When the paperbacks came out they no longer carried the advertisement for the Club, but this was briefly reinstated for the series that came out with the issue that had covers from the 1970s TV Series. The address in these books was given as the Darrell Waters one and the company that looked after Enid Blyton's copyright continued to send out the membership cards and badges until they finally closed the Club in September 1990.

On these pages, you can see some of the special memorabilia from the heydays of the club.

This is your membership card for the Famous Five Club, so please keep it safe. We hope you will like your badge and wear it whenever you can so that other members of the Club will recognise you. There are Famous Five members all over the world, so no matter where you are you will easily recognise and make friends with other members you meet.

The Famous Five Club has two aims, to make friends wherever you go and to help children who are ill or handicapped.

Enid Blyton herself always tried to help children in need and now we have started The Enid Blyton Trust for Children in order to continue her work. The Trust has already given money to serveral charities which are helping handicapped children to have a fuller life. Now the Trust is opening a National Library and Reading Information Centre for children whose handicap makes reading difficult.

Think how much you have enjoyed reading Enid Blyton's stories - your money will help other children to enjoy reading too!

THE

Enid Blyton

TRUST FOR CHILDREN

1. THIS WEEK'S NEWS of the Famous Five Club. Present members please note that the signal suggested by one of our boy-members, Roy Johnson, is the one mostly used. It is a quick raising of the right or left hand, and a quick opening and closing of the fingers. Five Fingers i.e., F.F. is a good signal for the Famous Five Club, because that, too, is F.F. for short. Please look on page 27 for the address of the Club and details. Any F.F. Club letters must ALWAYS be addressed there,

FIVE AND A HALF-TERM ADVENTURE

Here is another Famous Five short story for you to read and enjoy in one sitting.

The Five were at Kirrin Cottage for a short half-term holiday. For once, both the boys' school and the girls' school had chosen the same weekend!

'It hardly ever happens that we can spend half-term together,' said Anne, fondling Timmy. 'And what luck to have such lovely weather at the beginning of November!'

'Four days off!' said George. 'What shall we do?'

'BATHE!' said Julian and Dick together.

'What!' said their aunt, horrified, 'Bathe in November! You must be mad! I can't allow that, Julian, really I can't.'

'All right,' said Julian, grinning at his aunt. 'Don't worry. We haven't got our swimsuits here.'

'Let's walk over to Windy Hill,' said Dick. 'It's a grand walk, by the sea most of the way. And there may be blackberries and nuts still to find. I'd like a good walk.'

'Yes, let's do that,' said Anne. 'Aunt Fanny, shall we take a picnic lunch – or it is too much bother to prepare?'

'Not if you help me,' said her aunt, getting up. 'Come along – we'll see what we can find. But remember that it gets dark very quickly in the afternoon now, so don't leave it too late when you turn back.'

'Woof,' said Timmy at once, and put his big paw up on Dick's knee. He was always hoping to hear that magic word 'Walk!'

The Five set off half an hour later, with sandwiches and slices of fruit cake in a knapsack carried by Julian. Dick had a basket for any nuts or blackberries. His aunt had promised a blackberry-and-apple pie if they did find any berries for picking.

Timmy was very happy. He trotted along with the others, sniffing here and there, and barking at a curled-up hedgehog in a hole in a bank.

'Now, leave it alone,' said George. 'You really should have learnt by now that hedgehogs are not meant to be carried in your mouth, Timmy! Don't wake it up – it's gone to sleep for the winter!'

'It's a heavenly day for the beginning of November,' said Anne. 'The trees still have their leaves – all colours: red, yellow, brown, pink – and the beeches are the colour of gold.'

'Blackberries!' said Dick, catching sight of a bush whose sprays were still covered with the black fruit. 'I say – taste them – they're as sweet as sugar!'

As soon as the blackberries were to be seen on bushes here and there, the Five slowed up considerably! The blackberries that were still left were big and full of sweetness.

'They melt in my mouth!' said George. 'Try one, Timmy!' But Timmy spat the blackberry out in disgust.

'Manners, Timmy, manners!' said Dick at once, and Timmy wagged his big tail and pranced round joyfully.

It was a good walk but a slow one. They found a hazelnut copse and filled the basket with nuts that had fallen to the ground. Two red squirrels sat up in a nearby tree and chattered at them crossly. This was their nut copse!

'You can spare us a few!' called Anne. 'I expect you've got hundreds hidden away safely for the winter.'

They had their lunch on the top of Windy Hill. It was not a windy day, but, all the same, there was a good breeze on the top, and Julian decided to sit behind a big gorse bush for shelter.

'We'll be in the sun and out of the wind then,' he said. 'Spread out the lunch, Anne!' 'I feel terribly hungry!' said George. 'I can't believe it's only just one o'clock, Julian.'

'Well, that's what my watch says,' said Julian, taking a sandwich. 'Ha – ham and lettuce together – just what I like. Get away, Tim – I can't eat with you trying to nibble my sandwich too.'

It was a magnificent view from the top of the hill. The four children munched their sandwiches and gazed down into the valley below. A town lay there, comfortably sprawled in the shelter of the hills. Smoke rose lazily from the chimneys.

'Look – there's a train running along the railway-line down there,' said George, waving her sandwich in its direction. 'It looks just like a toy one.'

'It's going to Beckton,' said Julian. 'See – there's the station – it's stopping there. It really does look like a toy train!'

'Now it's off again – on its way to Kirrin,

I suppose,' said Dick. 'Any more sandwiches? What, none? Shame! I'll have a slice of cake, then – hand over, Anne.'

They talked lazily, enjoying being together again. Timmy wandered from one to the other, getting a titbit here and a scrap of ham there.

'I think I can see another nut copse over yonder – the other side of the hill,' said George. 'I vote we go and see what nuts we can find – and then I suppose we ought to be thinking of going back home. The sun is getting awfully low, Ju.'

'Yes, it is, considering it's only about two o'clock,' said Julian, looking at the red November sun hardly showing above the horizon. 'Come on, then – let's get a few more nuts, and then go back home. I love that long path winding over the cliffs beside the sea.'

They all went off to the little copse, and to their delight, found a fine crop of hazelnuts there. Timmy nosed about in the grass and brought mouthfuls of the nuts to George.

'Thanks, Timmy,' said George. 'Very clever of you – but I wish you could tell the bad ones from the good ones!'

'I say,' said Dick, after a while, 'the sun's gone, and it's getting dark. Julian, are you *sure* your watch is right?'

Julian looked at his watch. 'It says just about two o'clock still,' he said in surprise. 'Gosh – I must have forgotten to wind it up or something. It's definitely stopped now – and it must have been very slow before!'

'Ass,' said Dick. 'No wonder George thought it was long past lunch-time when you said it was one o'clock. We'll never get home before dark now – and we haven't any torches with us.'

'That cliff-path isn't too good to walk along in the dark, either,' said Anne. 'It goes so near the edge at times.'

'We'd better start back immediately,' said Julian. 'Awfully sorry about this – I never dreamed that my watch was wrong.'

'I tell you what would be a better idea,' said George. 'Why don't we just take the path down into Beckton and catch the train to Kirrin? We'll be so late if we walk back, and Mother will be ringing up the police about us!'

'Good idea of yours, George,' said Julian. 'Come on – let's take the path while we can still see. It leads straight down to the town.'

So away went the Five as fast as they could. It was dark when they reached the town, but that didn't matter, because the street lamps were alight. The made their way to the station, half-running down the main street.

'Look – there's *Robin Hood* on at the cinema here,' said Anne. 'Look at the posters!'

'And what's that on at the hall over there?' said George. 'Timmy, come here – oh, he's shot across the road. Come *HERE*, Timmy!'

But Timmy was running up the steps of the Town Hall. Julian gave a sudden laugh. 'Look – there's a big Dog Show on there – and old Timmy must have thought he ought to go in for it!'

'He smelt the dogs there,' said George, rather cross. 'Come on – let's get him, or we'll lose the next train.'

The hall was plastered with posters of dogs of all kinds. Julian stopped to read them while George went in after Timmy. Ah – here comes Tim again, looking very sorry for himself. I bet he knows he wouldn't win a single prize – except for brains!'

'It was the doggy smell that made him go to see what was on,' said George. 'He was awfully cross because they wouldn't let him in.'

'Some jolly valuable dogs here,' he said. 'Some beauties, too – look at the picture of this white poodle.

The train puffed in as they went to the booking-office for their tickets. The guard was blowing his whistle and waving his flag as they rushed on to the platform. Dick pulled open the door of the very last compartment and they all bundled in, panting.

'Hurry up – I think I can hear a train coming!' said Dick, and they all raced down the road to the station, which was quite near.

'Gosh – that was a near squeak,' said Dick, half-falling on to a seat. 'Look out, Tim – you nearly had me over.'

The four children got back their breath and looked round the carriage. It was not empty, as they had expected. Two other people were there, sitting at the opposite end, facing each other – a man and a woman. They looked at the Five, annoyed.

'Is she all right?' asked the man. 'Cover her up more – it's cold in here.'

'Oh,' said Anne, seeing the woman carrying a shawled bundle in her arms, 'I hope we haven't woken your baby. We only just caught the train.'

The woman rocked the little thing in her arms, and crooned to it, covering its head with a shawl – a rather dirty one, Anne noticed.

'There, there now,' crooned the woman, pulling the shawl tighter. The children lost interest and began to talk. Timmy sat still by George, very bored. Then he suddenly sniffed round, and went over to the woman. He leapt up on to the seat beside her and pawed at the shawl!

The woman shrieked and the man shouted at Timmy. 'Stop that! Get down! Here, you kids, look after that great dog of yours. It'll frighten the baby into fits!'

'Come here, Timmy,' said George at once, surprised that he should be interested in a baby. Timmy whined and went to George, looking back at the woman. A tiny whimpering noise came from the shawl, and the woman frowned. 'You've waked her,' she said, and began to talk to the man in a loud, harsh voice.

Timmy was very disobedient! Before George could stop him, he was up on the seat again, pawing at the woman and whining. The man leapt up furiously.

'Don't hit my dog, don't hit him, he'll snap at you!' shouted George – and mercifully, just at that moment the train drew in at a station.

'Whatever came over you, Tim?' she said 'You are never interested in babies!

Now sit down and don't move!'

Timmy was surprised at George's cross voice, and he crept under the seat and stayed there. The train came to a little station, where there was a small platform, and stopped to let a few people get out.

'Let's get out and go into another carriage,' said Anne, and opened the door. The four of them, followed by a most unwilling Timmy, were soon getting into a compartment near the engine. George looked crossly at Timmy.

'It's Seagreen Halt,' said Dick, looking out. 'And there go the man and woman and baby – I must say I wouldn't like them for a Mum and Dad!'

'It's quite dark now,' said George, looking through the window. 'It's a jolly good thing we just caught the train. Mother will be getting worried.'

It was nice to be in the cosy sitting-room at Kirrin Cottage again, eating an enormous tea and telling George's mother about their walk. She was very pleased with the nuts and blackberries. They told her about the man and woman and baby, too, and how funny Timmy had been, pawing at the shawl.

'He was *funny* before that,' said Anne, remembering. 'Aunt Fanny, there was a dog-show on at Beckton, and Timmy must have read the posters, and thought he could go in for it – because he suddenly dashed across the road and into the Town Hall where the show was being held!'

'*Really?*' said her aunt, laughing. 'Well, perhaps he went to see if he could find the beautiful little white Pekinese that was stolen there today! Mrs Harris rang up and told me about it – there was such a to-do. The little dog, which was worth five thousand pounds, was cuddled down in its basket one minute – and the next it was gone! Nobody was seen to take it, and though they hunted in every corner of the hall, there was no sign of the dog.'

'Gracious!' said Anne. 'What a mystery! How could anyone possibly take a dog like that away without being seen?'

'Easy,' said Dick. 'Wrap it in a coat, or pop it into a shopping basket and cover it up. Then walk through the crowd and out of the hall!'

'Or wrap it in a shawl and pretend it was a BABY – like the little one in that dirty shawl in the train,' said Anne. 'I mean – we thought that was a baby, of course – but it could easily have been a dog – or a cat – or even a monkey. We couldn't see its face!'

There was a sudden silence. Everyone was staring at Anne and thinking hard. Julian banged his hand on the table and made everyone jump.

'There's something in what Anne has just said,' he said. 'Something worth thinking about! BANG! Did anyone see even a glimpse of the baby's face– or hair? Did you, Anne – you were nearest?'

'No,' said Anne, quite startled. 'No, I didn't. I did try to see, because I like babies – but the shawl was pulled right over the face and head.'

'And I say – don't you remember how interested Timmy was in it?' said George, excited. 'He's never interested in babies – but he kept on jumping up and pawing at the shawl.'

'And do you remember how the baby whimpered?' said Dick. 'It was much more like

a little dog whining than a baby, now I come to think of it. No wonder Timmy was excited! He knew it was a dog by the smell!'

'Whew! I say – this is jolly exciting,' said Julian, getting up. 'I vote we go to Seagreen Halt and snoop round the tiny village there.'

'No,' said Aunt Fanny firmly. 'I will not have that, Julian. It's as dark as pitch outside, and I don't want you snooping round for dog thieves on your half-term holiday.'

'Oh, I say!' said Julian, bitterly disappointed.

'All right,' said Julian, sad to have a promising adventure snatched away so quickly. He went to the phone, frowning. Aunt Fanny might have let him and Dick slip out to Seagreen in the dark – it would have been such fun.

'Ring up the police,' said his aunt. 'Tell them what you have just told me – they'll be able to find out the truth very quickly. They will be sure to know who has a baby and who hasn't – they can go round snooping quite safely!'

The police were most interested and asked a lot of questions. Julian told them all he knew, and everyone listened intently. Then Julian put down the receiver and turned to the others, looking quite cheerful again.

'They were jolly interested,' he said. 'And they're off to Seagreen Village straight away in the police car. They're going to let us know what they find. Aunt Fanny – we CANNOT go to bed tonight till we know what happens!'

'No, we can't!' cried all the others, and Timmy joined in with a bark, leaping round excitedly.

'Very well,' said Aunt Fanny, smiling. 'What a collection of children you are – you can't even go for a walk without something happening! Now get out the cards and let's have a game.'

They played cards, with their ears listening for the ringing of the telephone bell. But it didn't ring. Supper time came and still it hadn't rung.

'It's no go, I suppose,' said Dick gloomily. 'We probably made a mistake.' Timmy suddenly began to bark, and then ran to the door, pawing at it.

'Someone's coming,' said George. 'Listen – it's a car!' They all listened, and heard the car stop at the gate – then footsteps came up the path and the front door bell rang. George was out in a trice, and opened it.

'Oh – it's the police!' she called. 'Come in, do come in.'

A burly policeman came in, followed by another. The second one carried a bundle in a shawl! Timmy leapt up to it at once, whining!

'Oh! It wasn't a baby, then!' cried Anne, and

the policeman smiled and shook his head. He pulled the shawl away – and there, fast asleep, was a tiny white Pekinese, its little snub nose tucked into the shawl!

'Oh – the darling!' said Anne. 'Wake up, you funny little thing!'

'It's been doped,' said the policeman. 'I suppose they were afraid of it whining in the night and giving its hiding-place away!'

'Tell us what happened,' begged Dick. 'Get down, Timmy. George, he's getting too excited – he wants the Peke to play with him!'

'Acting on your information we went to Seagreen,' said the policeman. 'We asked the porter what people got out of the train this evening, and if anyone carried a baby – and he said four people got out – and two of them were a man and woman, and the woman carried a baby in a shawl. He told us who they were – so away we went to the cottage . . .'

'Woof,' said Timmy interrupting, trying to get at the tiny dog again, but nobody took any notice of him.

'We looked through the back window of the cottage,' went on the policeman, 'and spotted what we wanted at once! The woman was giving the dog a drink of milk in a saucer – and she must have put some drug into it, because the little

thing dropped down and fell asleep at once while we were watching.'

'So in we went, and that was that,' said the second policeman, smiling round. 'The couple were so scared that they blurted out everything – how someone had paid them to steal the dog, and how they had taken their own baby's shawl, wrapped round a cushion – and had stolen the dog quite easily when the judging of the Alsatians was going on. They wrapped the tiny dog in the shawl, just as you thought, and caught the next train home!'

'I wish I'd gone to Seagreen Village with you,' said Julian. 'Do you know who told the couple to steal the little dog?'

'Yes – we're off to interview him now! He'll be most surprised to see us,' said the burly policeman. 'We've informed the owner that we've got her prize dog all right – but she feels so upset about it she can't collect it till the thing morning – so we wondered if you'd like to keep it for the night? Your Timmy can guard it, can't he?'

'Oh yes,' said George in delight. 'Oh, Mother – I'll take it to my room when I go to bed, and Timmy can guard the tiny thing as much as he likes. He'll love it!'

'Well – if your mother doesn't mind you having two dogs in your room, that's fine!' said the policeman, and signalled to the second one to give George the dog in the shawl. She took it gently, and Timmy leapt up again.

'No, Tim – be careful,' said George.

'Look what a tiny thing it is. You're to guard it tonight.'

Timmy looked at the little sleeping Pekinese, and then, very gently, he licked it with the tip of his pink tongue. This was the tiny dog he had smelt in the train, covered up in the shawl. Oh yes – Timmy had guessed at once

'I don't know what your name is,' said Dick, stroking the small silky head. 'But I think I'll call you Half-Term Adventure, though I don't know what that is in Pekinese!'

The two policemen laughed. 'Well, good night,

Madam, good night, children,' said the burly one. 'Mrs Fulton, the dog's owner, will call tomorrow morning for her Peke. He won a thousand-pound prize today – so I dare say you'll get some of that for a reward! Good night!'

The Five didn't want a reward, of course – but Timmy had one for guarding the little Peke all night. It's on his neck – the finest studded collar he has ever had in his life!

Good old Timmy!

FIVE GET INTO TROUBLE

Here's an intriguing extract from the eighth book in the series. It's the holidays and the Five have made a new friend in Richard. There's a rescue, a case of mistaken identity, and close encounters with villains ...

The four of them rode carefully down the rough, woodland path. They were glad when they came out into a lane.

Julian stopped for a moment to take his bearings. 'Now, according to the map, we ought to go to the right here then take the left at the fork some way down, and then circle a hill by the road at the bottom, and then ride a mile or two in a little valley till we come to the foot of Owl's Hill.'

'If we meet anyone we could ask them about Owl's Dene,' said Anne, hopefully.

'We shan't meet anyone out at night in this district!' said Julian. 'For one thing it's far from any village, and there will be no farmer, no policeman, no traveller for miles! We can't hope to meet anyone.'

The moon was up, and the sky cleared as they rode down the lane. It was soon as bright as day!

'We could switch off our lamps and save the batteries,' said Julian. 'We can see quite well now we're out of the woods and in the moonlight. Rather weird, isn't it?'

'I always think moonlight's strange, because although it shines so brightly on everything, you can never see much colour anywhere,' said Anne. She switched off her lamp too. She glanced down at Timmy. 'Switch off your head-lamps, Timmy!' she said, which made Richard give a sudden giggle. Julian smiled. It was nice to hear Anne being cheerful again.

'Timmy's eyes are rather like head-lamps, aren't they?' said Richard. 'I say – what about that food, Julian?'

'Right,' said Julian, and he fished in his basket. But it was very difficult to get it out with one hand, and try to hand it to the others.

'Better stop for a few minutes, after all,' he said at last. 'I've already dropped a hard-boiled egg, I think! Come on let's stack our bikes by the side of the road for three minutes, and gulp down something just to satisfy us for now.'

Richard was only too pleased. The girls were so hungry that they too thought it a good idea. They leapt off their bicycles in the moonlit road and went to the little copse at the side. It was a pine-copse, and the ground below was littered with dry brown pine-needles.

'Let's squat here for a minute or two,' said Julian. 'I say, what's that over there?'

Everyone looked. 'It's a tumbledown hut or something,' said George, and she went nearer to see. 'Yes, that's all – some old cottage fallen to bits. There's only part of the walls left. Rather an eerie little place.'

They went to sit down under the pine-trees. Julian shared out the food. Timmy got his bit too, though not so much as he would have liked! They sat there in the pine shadows, munching hungrily as fast as they could.

'I say, can anyone hear what I hear?'

said Julian, raising his head. 'It sounds like a car!'

They all listened. Julian was right. A car was purring quietly through the countryside! What a bit of luck!

'If only it comes this way!' said Julian. 'We could stop it and ask it for help. It could take us to the nearest police station at any rate!'

They left their food in the little copse and went to the roadside. They could see no head-lights shining anywhere, but they could still hear the noise of the car.

'Very quiet engine,' said Julian. 'Probably a powerful car. It hasn't got its head-lights on because of the bright moonlight.'

'It's coming nearer,' said George. 'It's coming down this lane. Yes – it is!'

So it was. The noise of the engine came nearer, and nearer. The children got ready to leap out into the road to stop the car. And then the noise of the engine died away suddenly.

The moon shone down on a big streamlined car that had stopped a little way down the lane. It had no lights at all, not even side-lights.

Julian put out his hand to stop the others from rushing into the road and shouting. 'Wait,' he said. 'This is just a bit strange!'

They waited, keeping in the shadows. The car had stopped not far from the tumbledown hut. A door opened on the off-side. A man got out and rushed across the road to the shadow of the hedge there. He seemed to be carrying a bundle of some kind.

A low whistle sounded. The call of an owl came back.

An answering signal! thought Julian, intensely curious about all this. I wonder what's happening? 'Keep absolutely quiet,' he breathed to the others. 'George, look after Timmy – don't let him growl.'

But Timmy knew when he had to be quiet. He didn't even give a whine. He stood like a statue, ears pricked, eyes watching the lane.

Nothing happened for a while. Julian moved very cautiously to the shelter of another tree, from where he could see better. He could see the tumbledown shack. He saw a shadow moving towards it from some trees beyond. He saw a man waiting – the man from the car probably. Who were they? What in the world could they be doing here at this time of night?

The man from the trees came at last to the man from the car. There was a rapid interchange of words, but Julian could not hear what they were. He was sure that the men had no idea at all that he and the other children were near. He cautiously crept to yet another tree, and peered from the shadows to try and see what was happening.

'Don't be long,' he heard one man say. 'Don't bring your things to the car. Stuff them down the well.'

Julian could not see properly what the man was doing, but he thought he must be changing his clothes. Yes, now he was putting on the others – probably from the bundle the first man had brought from the car. Julian was more and more curious. What a funny business! Who was the second man? A refugee? A spy?

The man who had changed his clothes now picked up his discarded ones and

went to the back of the shack. He came back without them, and followed the first man across the lane to the waiting car.

Even before the door had closed, the engine was purring, and the car was away! It passed by the pine-copse where the children were watching, and they all shrank back as it raced by. Before it had gone very far it was travelling very fast indeed.

Julian joined the others. 'Well, what do you make of all that?' he said. 'Funny business, isn't it? I watched a man

changing his clothes – goodness knows why. He's left them somewhere at the back of the shack – down a well, I think I heard them say. Shall we see?'

'Yes, let's,' said George, puzzled. 'I say, did you see the number on the car. I only managed to spot the letters – KMF.'

'I saw the numbers,' said Anne. '102. And it was a black Bentley.'

'Yes. Black Bentley, KMF 102,' said Richard. 'Up to some funny business, I'll be bound!'

ANSWERS

FIVE GO TO BILLYCOCK HILL PUZZLE

Across
1. Hill
6. Trip
7. Nobody
9. Peculiar
12. Caves
13. Place
14. Stormy
17. Night
19. Spider
20. Morning
21. Butterfly

Down
2. Look
3. Pool
4. Happened
5. Trouble
8. Janes
10. News
11. Knows
12. Camping
15. Annoyed
16. Jeff
18. Through

NAME SQUARE

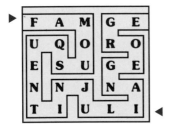

SPOT THE DIFFERENCE

The telescope has been drawn the wrong way round.

THE FIENDISH FAMOUS FIVE QUIZ

1. Aunt Fanny.
2. Mr Wilton and Mr Thomas.
3. Alf, the fisherboy (a bonus point if you said Alf and James, as in some editions of the books he is given both names!)
4. Joanna.
5. Miss Peters.
6. Two pythons.
7. Guy and Harry Lawdler.
8. Henrietta, who likes to be called Henry.

9. Deep grooves carved into the wall to be used as a sort of ladder for anyone climbing down the hole.
10. Very Important People.
11. A long metal bar flattened at one end used as a lever to lift stones etc.
12. The Catacombs.
13. Timmy, while looking for a way into the castle.
14. It leads to the site of the ancient Roman camp on the common.
15. Red Tower.
16. It is a signal that a prisoner has escaped.
17. Sand.
18. She ties one end of a length of thin string to their tent flaps and the other end to her big toe. Then when the string is pulled it will wake her up!
19. He hides in the boot of the car when it is about to leave the house and then escapes after the car has stopped.
20. They find chocolate paper on the floor.
21. They find a trail of spilt oil leading up the stairs to the tower room.
22. Yan.
23. He removes the rope that they needed to climb out of the cave.
24. Dobby and Trotter.
25. A thorn.

GUESS WHO?

1. George; 2. Timothy; 3. Julian; 4. Dick; 5. Julian; 6. Anne; 7. Timothy; 8. Anne; 9. Julian; 10. George; 11. Dick; 12. Julian

ANOTHER MYSTERY AT MYSTERY MOOR

12. WARILY
5. HEADACHE
4. STABLE
2. HENRY
13. NOISE
14. PLEASED
16. TERRIBLE
20. MORNING
10. PATRIN
19. GOOD
13. NIGHT
7. GEORGE
15. STARTLING
21. MYSTERY

The message reads, WE ARE PRISONERS, and it was written by George.

FIVE GO ADVENTURING FIND-A-WORD

The answer is Enid Blyton and her name is repeated 6 times in the puzzle.

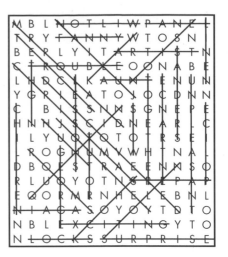

ACKNOWLEDGEMENTS

Meet the Baddies and the Fiendish Famous Five Quiz © Norman Wright, 2000, and adapted from The Famous Five: Everything You Ever Needed to Know.

Who Are the Famous Five and Name Square first appeared in Enid Blyton's Adventure Magazine No. 14.

The TV stills from the 1978 and 1995 TV shows are reproduced courtesy of Coolabi.

The cartoon strip version of Five Have Plenty of Fun first appeared in Enid Blyton's Adventure Magazine No. 11.

Meet Eileen Soper, Sunny Stories, and The Famous Five Club © Tony Summerfield, 2014.

Food in the Famous Five © Josh Sutton, 2012. This piece first appeared on the Guardian newspaper website.

Five Go to Smuggler's Top first appeared in Mystery and Suspense, issue 9.

The illustrations from Five and a Half-Term Adventure first appeared in The Big Enid Blyton Book.

Special thanks to Kristopher McKie of Seven Stories (www.sevenstories.org.uk) for supplying the images included in Behind the Scenes.